The 5 Wise Grandchildren

By
Dyan Beyer

Illustrated by: Carolee Carrara

Scripture quotations marked NIV are taken from the *Holy Bible, New International Version®. NIV®*. Copyright © 1973, 1978, 1984 by International Bible Society. Used by permission of HYPERLINK "http://www.zondervan.com/" Zondervan. All rights reserved. [Biblica]

To order additional copies of this book, contact:
Xlibris
844-714-8691
www.Xlibris.com
Orders@Xlibris.com

ISBN: Softcover   978-1-6698-4710-6
       Hardcover   978-1-6698-4814-1
       EBook   978-1-6698-4706-9

Print information available on the last page

Rev. date: 03/31/2023

This book is dedicated to my five grandchildren.

George

Bear

Grace

Paul

Creed

With love and prayers that you will always trust in God and in return, receive great wisdom.

Proverbs 3:13: Blessed are those who find wisdom, those who gain understanding.

nce upon a time there were five grandchildren who liked to play and go out to different places with their Nonnie Gram. Whenever they were with her, they would ask for something and Nonnie Gram would give it to them because she loved them so much!

"Nonnie Gram, can we have an ice-cream cone?" asked George.

And Nonnie Gram would always ask, "Would you rather have an ice-cream cone or would you rather have wisdom?"

The five grandchildren would always choose the ice-cream cone.

"Oh, Nonnie Gram, look at all the toys! Can we have them?" all five grandchildren asked.

Nonnie Gram smiled and asked her question, "Would you rather have toys or would you rather have wisdom?"

"We want toys, Nonnie Gram!" all five shouted out always choosing the toys.

Nonnie Gram and the five grandchildren were taking a walk when they saw Mr. Smith and his dog. They loved playing with, Fanny, the Cocker Spaniel. All five grandchildren started asking Nonnie Gram if they could get a puppy!

"Would you rather have a puppy or would you rather have wisdom?" Nonnie Gram asked.

"We want the puppy!" shouted the grandchildren.

The next day Nonnie Gram bought them a ruby colored Cocker Spaniel puppy who they named, Scarlett.

There was one special park that Nonnie Gram would take the five grandchildren to. It was their favorite place to go on Saturdays.

"I'm going to climb the monkey bars!" said Bear.

"This time, Nonnie Gram, I'm going down the big slide," said Grace.

"I want to go on the swing!" said Creed.

"I want to go on the see-saw!" said Paul.

"Not me! I want to play in the tree house!" said George.

Once George mentioned the tree house, the other grandchildren all at once started saying, "Yeah, the tree house is the best! Nonnie Gram, can you buy us a tree house?"

Nonnie Gram smiled and asked them, "Would you rather have a tree house or would you rather have wisdom?"

They all answered together, "The tree house, the tree house!"

The next Saturday was a rainy day so the five grandchildren couldn't go to the park. They played with Scarlett all morning and then asked if Nonnie Gram would take them to see a movie.

"Would you rather go to the movies or would you rather have wisdom?" Nonnie Gram asked them.

They all answered exactly as Nonnie Gram expected.

"The movies! We rather go to the movies!" the grandchildren shouted out.

In the summertime, Nonnie Gram would take the five grandchildren to the beach. They loved to play in the sand and swim in the ocean but most of all they loved looking for shells!

Grace would always find the prettiest shell. George would find the funniest looking shell. Paul would find the most colorful shell. Creed would find the biggest shell. Bear would find the most shells!

"Nonnie Gram, we need some new shovels and pails for the beach," said the grandchildren.

"Do you think so?" asked Nonnie Gram.

"YES, YES, YES!" shouted George, Bear, Grace, Paul and Creed.

"Would you rather have new shovels and pails or would you rather have wisdom?" Nonnie Gram asked them.

"Shovels and pails! Nonnie Gram, shovels and pails!" the five grandchildren shouted out.

On the way home from the beach Nonnie Gram stopped in front of the bicycle store. The grandchildren's eyes opened wide when they realized where they were.

"Are you going to buy us each a bicycle, Nonnie Gram?"

"If that is what you want but I rather you choose wisdom," Nonnie Gram replied.

The five grandchildren became very quiet and then they asked, "What is wisdom, Nonnie Gram?"

"The next time we go to the park, I will tell you."

"Nonnie Gram, now that we are at the park, can you tell us what wisdom is?"

"Wisdom allows you to use knowledge correctly so you make better choices and decisions. Having wisdom protects us," Nonnie Gram explained.

"But what is it?" the five grandchildren asked curiously.

Nonnie Gram smiled as she took out her Bible and placed it on the table before saying, "Wisdom is something that is better than ice cream, better than any toy, any pet, any shell, any tree house, any movie, any shovel or pail, and better than any bike. Wisdom is even better than gold and silver!" Nonnie Gram said excitedly.

"How do you get wisdom?" asked George.

"You ask for wisdom from God and you ask Him faithfully and humbly. When you read the Bible you will know our Lord better," Nonnie Gram said happy that the grandchildren were listening.

"If we do those things, will we get wisdom?" asked Bear.

"Yes, asking God is the first step in receiving wisdom. God's wisdom is the blessing from God. His blessing helps us to use our knowledge," Nonnie Gram said.

"Can you teach us wisdom, Nonnie Gram?" asked Grace.

"No, I can't teach you wisdom. Although, knowledge can be taught and with knowledge you have the ability to make good judgments but you need wisdom to use that knowledge. That's why wisdom is so important to have."

"Can God teach us wisdom?" asked Paul.

"Yes. The Word of God teaches us wisdom," answered Nonnie Gram.

"Can you buy us wisdom?" asked Creed.

Nonnie Gram smiled, "No, you can't buy wisdom. Wisdom comes from God. It's a gift from Him."

"And what do we do with wisdom if we get it?" asked the five grandchildren.

Nonnie Gram waited until the grandchildren stopped asking questions and then she said, "You use it! God's wisdom can make one wise man more powerful than ten rulers in a city. Wisdom saves the life for those who have it. Wisdom gives joy, health, long life, peace, honor, and riches. Wisdom makes you a better person and gives you a happier life!"

The five grandchildren listened carefully to what Nonnie Gram was explaining. They started to understand how important wisdom was and how important it was to ask God for it.

"Nonnie Gram, why didn't you tell us about wisdom before?" asked the grandchildren.

"Because you weren't ready to understand what wisdom is. You weren't old enough to want to know so I waited for you to ask. And that, my five grandchildren, is the beginning of wisdom! We will grow in wisdom when we obey God."

They waited for Nonnie Gram to ask her usual question and when she didn't, they asked her.

"Nonnie Gram, would you rather have gold and silver or would you rather have wisdom?"

Nonnie Gram smiled and answered, "I would rather have wisdom. Now, I will ask the five of you one very important question."

The five grandchildren waited with open eyes to hear Nonnie Gram's question.

"What would you rather have more than anything else?"

And all five grandchildren shouted out, "WISDOM!"

"Now I have five very WISE grandchildren," Nonnie Gram said smiling.

The End

How much better to get wisdom than gold, to get insight rather than silver!
Proverbs 16:16

Printed in the United States
by Baker & Taylor Publisher Services